THE GARDEN of GASSY

"This is our amazing garden!" said Emma and Sam.

"There are carrots and beets, tomatoes and yams."

"We grew them ourselves, from little seeds.

We've watered and watched and pulled all the weeds."

When we checked on our plants like we do every day,
we found three gnomes had come here to stay!

"Well hello to you little gnomes.
You're welcome to make this garden your home."

Everything was going well
then from the garden came a smell.

Emma looked down and what did she see?
The gnomes were having a party for three!

The gnomes were all dancing but that wasn't all.

"This just won't do!" cried Emma and Sam.
"These gnomes are going to have to scram!
All those smelly toots will ruin our crop.
We need all that tooting and farting to stop!"

So they moved the gnomes to the pear tree.
"Now you stay here, gnome one two and three!"

That didn't stop the gnomes, not one bit!
They raced back to the garden - lickity split!

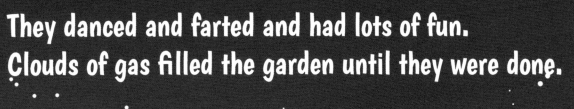

They danced and farted and had lots of fun.
Clouds of gas filled the garden until they were done.

The children saw that the gnomes had returned and those stinky farts were their biggest concern.

So they moved the gnomes and added a sign.
Gnomes are NOT welcome - not of any kind!

The gnomes hiked back and laughed at the signs.
They went back to farting and dancing in line.

The children were puzzled, sad and perplexed.
They tried to figure out what to do next.

"This is tricky." Emma said with a sigh.
"We need a fence and it had better be high."
So they spent all day making a fence made of sticks.
"This should stop them...even with all their tricks!"

The gnomes couldn't get into the garden that night
and all the next week they stayed out of sight.

Emma and Sam thought they had won.
They had solved the gnome problem,
their work here was done.

But while Emma cheered with a dance and a song,
Sam noticed that something was wrong.

All of their plants were being devoured by bugs!
There were beetles, moths, grasshoppers and slugs!

The leaves all had holes and the carrots were chewed.
"Oh no!" said Sam. "There goes our food!"

"I think those gnomes are misunderstood, maybe they do our garden some good."

So down to the garden they snuck that night
to talk to the gnomes about their plight.

"What happened to our garden little gnomes?
Do your farts hurt our plants? We need to know!"

"Oh no!" said the gnomes. "That's not going on!
We protect your garden - from dusk to dawn!
All that dancing and farting that just looks like
play is keeping all the bad bugs away!"

"We're sorry that we got it all wrong!
Please help our garden grow healthy and strong!"

So the gnomes went back to work every night
and tooted and danced until things were right.

Now the tomatoes are plump and the corn is tall and Emma and Sam are enjoying it all.

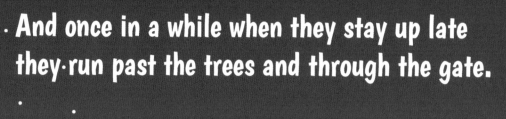

And once in a while when they stay up late
they·run past the trees and through the gate.

They giggle and dance and toot here and there as they dance with the gnomes in the stinky night air.

These are some of the harmful insects that might be in a vegetable garden.
Did you find them in the story?

cutworm moth

cabbage moth

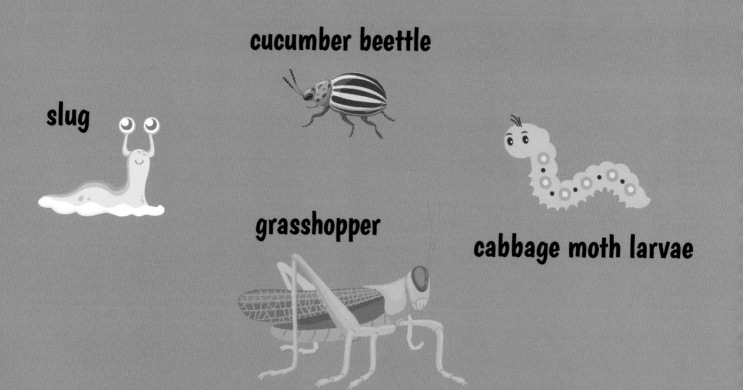

cucumber beetle

slug

grasshopper

cabbage moth larvae

These are some of the beneficial insects that might be in a vegetable garden.
Did you find them in the story?

bee

dragonfly

ladybug

ground beetle

praying mantis

Gardeners know that if you encourage the good bugs to live in your garden, they'll control the bad bugs. And of course, a gnome or two will help. (:

Printed in Great Britain
by Amazon